TWIST AND TURN

OF THE HEIST

THE ASSISTED LIVING CAPERS

Samantha Dala

Printed in the United States of America
Library of Congress Control Number: 2022923029
ISBN: Softcover   979-8-88622-858-8
             e-Book   979-8-88622-859-5
Republished by: PageTurner Press and Media LLC
Publication Date: 01/05/2023

To order copies of this book, contact:
PageTurner Press and Media
Phone: 1-888-447-9651
info@pageturner.us
www.pageturner.us

TWIST AND TURN OF THE HEIST

OF THE HEIST

THE ASSISTED LIVING CAPERS

This is just Another Story to be told by Dee.

There will be no cases solved till the end of this book. That is why it is called the twist and turns of the heist. Please keep reading, it gets better and better as the book goes on.

Me: Well I was brought into this place that I would not bring anyone to. It has very bad carpet with stains on the rug. Like someone took a dump in the middle of it, and I have pictures of here when I moved in. This place is where crime is always going on and I know who they are,

And yet no one can figure out who is taking what don't belong to them.

They even have cameras, but they are not pointed at what is taking place at the time of the crime. So guess who is on the job? Good ole Dee, I am always where I need to be.

And yet no one has been caught. That is because I was not here before. I am the best Detective in the state, and I have a great reputation because I know what I am doing and where to look.

I have been here for about 3 months and I have figured out who is good and who is not but being robbed of something out of your room, don't work for me. So I am here and on the job, because I love my job it is never dull.

I guess that is why I can never retire because when you are called the best then retirement is not heard of. Being in this old folk's home is just a plan from someone higher up,

I have never been in a place like this before so I am going to show these people how to solve a case. And the best way to do this is to do it on my own, and I will never hurt anyone.

To me everyone gets a second chance, no matter what.

That is always my way of doing things. Sam's Detective Agency's owner and the writer and producer, of my own books, no one else.

See when I got put in here I thought it was for a rest. That was a joke. It turned out to be a case of hot fingers,

But no one bothered to tell me this, I had to see it for myself.

I do have some close friends in here and I will tell you later who they are. Just hold on I said I'd tell you in time just not quite yet, okay?

I have noticed that I am not working with my kids today, they don't even know where I am, because no one told them anything,

I have asked for something like coffee and they ask if I want anything else, and I say no but thank you for asking,

You are most welcome ma'am,

This is a proper way of saying something nice to the help,

They were very nice people,

Wow that is way too cool for me to do something like that and then being proper, not in this lifetime.

(E) says,,;

I have made it a long time not being proper and that is never going to change,

Ok well let me know if you ever want to change ok,

I sure will but don't hold your breath, ok,

I am going for a walk and look and see whatever I can do ,wow the view from the back yard is amazing, birds are singing and the trees are all in bloom,

See I have my own ways of doing things I am a Detective after all,

I always go all out on my cases, where most Detectives don't,

But I do get the job done and it is always the right way,

Because when you go all out you find things that you might have overlooked before.

But I am a one of a kind Detective,

And I have about 36 people working for me and we are always busy, I have had my team for about 52 years or so and we are like family.

A lot of workers don't have families so Christmas is a lot of fun for me. I can buy gifts and no one knows what I am getting for them. Christmas is a mystery to most of my worker's. I think if I ever got sick my team could do my job for me.

Cause I have trained them all myself, so I know they could handle a case by themselves and they are always here for me and I am always here for them to see if you have to go to a seen more than one time, then you are doing something wrong, I always do it right the first time, One time and I figure it out.

I have never been here more than one time and I have never been wrong, well not yet anyway, and I am not looking forward too ever being wrong, I am a Detective and a CSI, so I have my work cut out for me.

I have been told I am the best Detective in

the State and that is California and Oregon, so that is 2 States, I am so proud of my work, and all my people. We are a team that no one can ever split up.

Ok on with my job I have been here for a while now and I have 5 people that are working with just a dimwit, her name is E and she is as dumb as they get, she is always walking around like she has a cob up her butt and that look on her face, is enough to kill.

She is something else. I can't use names but I can use litters.

E: Is just a pain in the butt.

C: Is nice to you but she will stab you in the back and say something like it wasn't me.

D: He is in an electric wheelchair and yet he steels anything he can and he don't care.

Then there is Switch hitter. She is just as dumb as they come and she is very good at being that way and she has a fetish with bottles and cans.

She has to know where they go and if they are going to a good place.

Shuffles then we have a mummy that walk around all night and her harsh voice. Hi how are you, and she keeps on walking.

D S: Well then we have one person in here that likes to be heard on the workers all the time.

The time he yells at all the staff people all the time,

Just to show what an ass he is, D S, is his name,

Me: Ok enough about these weird people let's get on with the cases at hand.

Ok, it all started a few months ago when I first got here and something was mentioned about me being a friend to someone in here.

And I said yes I am and so it begins.

A friend told me that someone got into her apartment and took some Jewelry and did not ask to even see what any of it looked like.

But the guy was moving from one apartment to another and things started coming up missing,

C: Said I know where all your jewelry is, and it was not me that took it.

Me: But she is wearing a lot of new rings on her hands,

Gee I wonder where it all came from guy's dead wife, but yet he don't say anything about it to her at all.

So she got away with taking all the jewelry. He is a dummy when it comes to these odd ladies here.

H J: Then we have a drunk here that is a person that does drugs and he is a full time drunk and he will do anything to get his beer but that is just the way he is because he has to have his drinks.

Then we have the cloths that disappear after the move from one room to another. Can you guess where all those went, well not to her family.

E: Got it all and that is just a part of this Caper.

Just like I said early on, this guy, he is just so blind he is like a dog in heat.

D S: Has anyone seen my TV remotes? I can't find them anywhere someone took them. I guess I have to buy some more and see how long they will stay in my apartment.

Me: He sure does have a time with his TV remote. If he would look in the drunk's apartment he would find what he is looking for. Or even go to E apartment and search and he might find more than what he is searching for.

But that might be just too much to handle for him, he is blind when it comes to E. She is his girlfriend, yuck but it is. Any way the search is on and he knows nothing about it because he would tell his girlfriends and that might get messy.

And I do my job the right way not where you have to come back all the time that is the wrong way, I have a couple of friends that come to visit me every now and again.

Me, S and L. They are on my team they are married and they are quite the team.

I just wish I could see them a little more often than I do now, but we all work some odd hours but we are all very happy in what we do for a living because we catch the bad people that is our joy in life.

D S: Is always bitching about something missing and yet he lets E in his apartment then he says he has money missing.

You know I just thought of something, maybe she planted for someone else because when she and Switch hitter are around things go bye bye and it is not noticeable until after they are out of sight, go figure right, these people are something else.

Well my step daughter is coming in to help me with writing down everything that has come up missing but she is an undercover writer for me, and she is great at it.

She has done a few of my books for me, she reads them and she tells me what is missing in it. So you see I trust her, she is great, Grace has been doing this for about 16 years for me.

And she is almost as good at writing these as I am, but I am the one spending the money and no one else. So if I need someone on a spare of a moment I will call her, she is family and the best person for watching over things.

All I have to do for her is tell her where I am on a case and she knows where to go from there. She knows me so we'll we just have a good time together so we can do our jobs.

We always have more than one going at a time, and so we are all working at the same time and in different places which makes it better on all of us. We have capers all over the U S. And Canada, we are traveling people.

And being a Detective you have to love to travel because that is what we do most. And we always get the bad person, male or female.

Grace: If it was not for her I would not have a great job like this. I was not working with anyone else but I just thought why not I need a job and rent money, so I applied and got this job

And I love it so much and so does Alisha, she is so happy all the time. She watches everything I do and she tries to do it just like I did.

And believe it or not she is better at something than I am, now that is saying something, She is only Eleven years young and she is my best helper and she is my only child, one is enough for anyone, So she is doing odds and ends for me even on the farm.

And she will exercise the horses for me that is a job all in itself, so doing this case for the twist and turns of the heist #2: The Assisted Living Capers,

It is all about these crazy people in this place and how stupid they are. This is not the book yet it is just a rough idea of what you are going to read.

I am from California and I have all the best Detective from here.

I have trained all my people, that is why they are the best and I think if I ever got sick, my team could do my jobs for me.

And it would be like I am there, they would do things the way I do things. Just the Fax ma'am just the fax, and just one shot only that is all I ever need, if you have to go back and do it again then somethings wrong.

It should not take any longer than 7 hours to do one crime area no matter what you say, evidence is evidence, and that is that. Otherwise, you are not doing a good job.

The longer you take the more evidence you have to solve the case. I am the voice of experience after a few years under your belt you learn these things and so do all the people on my team, and I also taught my team CSI.

Training for the team work, and they are all still with me.

So I guess I did a good job. I have never heard anything bad about the CSI training.

See, once you learn the CSI training then you have what you need for this case.

And on with what you have learned so fare you don't want someone else getting the blame for something they did not do.

To me that would be wrong. I have been touch with a friend of mine that is in an old folk's home and that someone is stealing things, they also have Cameras and yet nobody gets caught.

My thoughts, are the cameras even working, because if they are not working then there is a lawsuit just waiting to happen, that place can be sued.

So I put myself in here to catch the bad

people that are doing wrong to other people. To me this should be easy, cause I like all kinds of people, that is just who I am. It takes all kinds to make this world go around, and I do mean all kinds.

In this place you see all kind of people, small, short, tall, big, and just plain people like me. I am no different than anyone in here well other than being a detective.

I don't steal from other people but some of these people do. I am sure I know who is making things disappear, but I'm not going to say who till the end. Sorry, If you can figure it out then you can be a good person to have figured it out on your own.

In the meantime just read on and you can guess where this is going, okay.

I can say it is not going back to the beginning because that is what you are reading know, it is like the movie CLUES.

I have come across some good people in

here and there are some that need to be taken out to the woodshed and beaten till they can learn some respect for you.

I have met quite a few people here, and some of them are nice and some are assholes, but me I am just me. I will never change, I have some friends outside of here that have given up on me.

There is one family that made sure of making sure that I was homeless, and that is another reason I am in this place, God I hate this place.

This place has so many things wrong with it the owners will never get it all fixed up and I have never heard of anyone saying it was a place for mother or father.

I went to the store the other day and they did not even know I was gone and the reason I went was because I didn't want to ask anyone for help.

It was just a milk run for me and I enjoyed getting out for a while because I feel like I am in prison, the only thing missing is the Bar's on the windows.

Assisted living is a joke, they don't assist you in anything in here. They do alcohol and drugs in here and no one will do anything about it. The cops here are a joke they will not even try and find them in here.

They might miss a donut break and that would just ruin their day. When a person is found dead in the room what are the cops going to do? Just sweep it under the rug, if I did not have to pay money for living here in this small room. It is less than 200 foot, the state pay for most of it and they are getting the shaft because this place should have been closed down a longtime ago.

The people that are stealing wine glasses and silverware and plates. Whatever they want, whatever they're looking for they will find.

I can say if you are looking for something go to the room that smells like crap all the time, and you will find some of what has legs and walked away.

You can also find clothes and sodas that she did not buy she just takes whatever she wants, no if and but about it.

And she has a smart ass attitude about it, we will call her Switch hitter girl, this sure fits her to a tee.

But the people here really are a piece of work, if you can find them working that would be a switch, I don't think it is in their paperwork.

The old owners had these cameras put up and anything that goes wrong is never on the cameras for some reason, and get this, no sound on the cameras either.

There is something wrong with this picture, people can see you going up and down the halls but that is all, so the people who are stealing are very lucky because the cameras are not watching you.

People in here are on a fixed income, and yet they are getting ripped off.

The state will not do anything and the owners are too busy spending the money from here on another building and that is called laundering money and that is Illegal if you get caught that is jail time for everyone involved.

But I don't care I am moving. I hope very soon, and this place has new owners. We did have a drug dealer in here but now he is gone he killed one person and he was just in his 50's and that is young, but he got away with it.

When I first got here I met a guy that liked forensic files and he said;

"Can you solve that before the end of the show?"

"I said, sure and I did, and he was so amazed I had it solved before the ending."

"Wow! How did you know that someone else was involved just by watching?"

"I am a CSI agent and a detective so it was easy for me, I said."

Someone came into the TV room and said I want to watch something else. I said no we are watching this right now, you can have the TV in just about 12 minutes, okay?

So we finish watching our program when it was over we said we are all finished.

So have a great night, and we left the room, he turned on the news for about 5 minutes and left, but I have some friends in here that like to play dice.

I have some cool people around and they taught me how to play a dice game called 10 thousand, it is a great game,

I am very glad I met these people, it keeps me out of trouble and sane I think.

But I am still in this place and I wish I was somewhere else like my own home (not Oregon).

I just have nowhere else to go back to thanks to DH he is someone that I would put in jail. And let the inmates have their way.

But I am still doing my thing in this place and yes I have it all figured out. This place is so fare out of control it is funny because no one knows what each other is going to do so they just do whatever they want and no one says anything.

Some of these people are so far out there that they will never be able to look back. That is what drinking does to you, you look like a spaced out nut.

There is 3 females in here that like taking things that don't belong to them but they don't care, it is their stuff now.

Then we have a guy here that thinks he is a ladies man he thinks he is hot and in a wheelchair and he is living with the biggest pain in the ass that is in this place.

We call him the male whore of assisted living and that is mild for what we really think.

AC can be a nice guy but what a pain in the butt he is, and with switch hitters around he can be a total ass.

When the switch hitter is not around he is a totally different person. He makes passes at all the women that come here.

But that is just A C.

And we have dogs in here and you would think that they would let you know when you have a praller coming to your door.

Just to give you a heads up to be prepared. That someone is at the door that should not be there so this person will be in for a surprise when you open the door.

But catching a thief in here is a joke because the constables will never do anything. They are chicken so they will slap her on the hand and let her do what she wants.

Her name is (shuffles) she just walks baby steps up and down the hallway all hours of the day and night and yet no one says anything about it because she is not all there. I was making a tie blanket one day and I had a Pepsi on the table and she came in took my Pepsi and left she did not say a word.

But most of the people in here are not all here. We do have one in here that thinks she is queen bee and she is the biggest thief in here and she will take something while you are watching.

And that is big ass D C. She thinks since she has been here over 6 years she can tell everyone what to do and where to go, wrong.

But all she is, a slut out for anything that wears pants. Well I found out we had some ones place broken into last night and yet the cameras seen nothing.

Why do we have cameras if they don't work that is so stupid.

I had a neighbor that had something taken from his room and he said something but they did nothing.

"What is wrong with these people are they all mentally unstable or what?"

Like I said before there are so many thieves in here, you will have quite a time naming them all.

I have a friend named Shi who knows who I am and she knows what I do, and she knows that I have never been in a place like this before and she is never going to tell anyone what I have been doing for my book. She is a good sport and she is my best friend and she always will be. There is no one on this earth any better than her. She likes my books she said they are good so I hope she likes this one too.

I want out of this place and back where I belong in California. I just want to go back to work full time then you don't have to worry about anything but what you are working on at that time.

You don't get old before your time, hell I am old now I hate to think about getting much older, but as long as I have my books I am fine and my Detective Agency and all my workers, hey! I am great.

And my jobs just keep coming in,

But this job here is like no other job I have ever done before and it is quite something because you never know who is going to do something stupid next.

But with the people in here it is a toss-up who is not on first here. It is whoever the dumbstruck first is, and believe me there is a line but I always know who will be first.

Switch hitter is first in the line, she is the one that thinks all the guys are here for her. Then there is shuffles she is second in line, then there is D C.

If she don't get what she wants she writes notes and that she has priorities here cause she has been here longer than anyone. She is wrong there are two ladies that have been here over 20 years so she needs to think again.

But as usual I know who has been here longer than she has, good ole lady carol and Carleen, they have been here for 20 years. They are the sweetest ladies that I have ever met.

But they don't tell you that there are other people here that have been here a lot longer than them.

Slut herself, D C, has only been here 6 years.

I think that if people were smarter there wouldn't be a problem with this place they need to upload the cameras and get better people in here.

I say this because this place is about to hit rock bottom and I don't see it making it back on the green side any time soon because they don't know how to run a place like this.

They need to do background checks on the people that are coming here to work and on the people that they are putting in here, that right there is a big must.

This place is not for me it is for people that do not have too much wrong with them because assisted living is a big farce because they do not assist you in anything that I know of.

They say something just to get you in here

and that is as far as it goes. All you have to do is ask some of the people that are in here already and they will tell you the same thing I have told you.

Well when I got in here it was not because of the food because that is nothing to brag about. I fix my own food in my room and I love my cooking.

I have seen some of their food and tasted it, this will never happen again, their food is yuck.

In all I am not happy in here, I know who has done all this stealing here but no one wants to believe me. I know who and I would be willing to bet that I could show you where everything is at.

But they keep telling me that I don't know.

They are wrong, I know everything that is missing where everything belongs. They don't want to know anything because they are total morons and they are not all here yet but we know who they are.

The people who think they are running this place is a joke, all of them are and that is just the way I feel. I always thought that we were all created equal but not in here you are all just in here for this place to get money from the state but some of us don't want to be here.

We have a family but that is not what we all want, we want to be on our own, if we can.

I for one have family in California and that is where I want to be. I am not a spring chicken anymore but I want to be home where I do belong.

I have been here long enough to see people go out on a stretcher and they never came back. Not only do I have a case of missing objects now I have another case of who brought in the COVID and I know who did the first case but it was three or more people and it started with the med tech here.

People here are so blind to see that it is the staff bringing it to this place and I got it from the med tech, then when I wanted to go the hospital they would not call for me. I had to call the hospital just for an ambulance to take me there and they told me I had about 1 hour left. I went in the hospital on the 2nd of November 2021 and I got back here on the 7th of November 2021.

That was a very scary thing to go through alone but I did, and as far as I am concerned I never want to do it again but while I was in the hospital I figured out some of the things that came up missing. When your mind will not turn off then you have to go with the flow

And that is what I did, I have never been in a position like this before so it was like a challenge to me and I love challenges.

It is just who I am in my life the more challenging the better it is for me because it makes my mind work better. That is why I am still working on my cases and my books, and I never give up on anything I start that is not my way.

C B: Knock, knock, and knock on my door

Me: Yes? May I help you?

C B: It's me. CB

Me: May I help you with something?

C B: I was just in my room and someone just came in and took my porcelain dolls and it was all 3 that she took but they are antiques so I can't get any more of them, So what can I do about that?

Me: Well let's see where we're you at this time.

C B: In my shower.

Me: Wow that is gutsy was your door locked or did you left it unlock?

C B: It was unlocked because I was home and my dog did not even bark.

Me: So it was someone you know and the dog likes. How many people do you let in to your place that the dog likes?

C B: Well, maybe 3 at most I think. He was

raised around most of these people so he knows who he likes and who he don't like.

Me: What about the guy that has most of his stuff stolen?

C B: You mean D S? He is such an ass at times. I don't see him coming to my place taking dolls unless he thought they were his ex-wife's dolls.

Me: Well that makes sense to me but why just go in to your room. Why not just ask you about the dolls. That would make more sense than just taking them.

C B: I have no idea but I was thinking I had my dog in my shower with me so no one was in the front room. That is why the dog did not bark he was with me in the bathroom.

Me: Ok well we know you were just in the room but you saw the door part way open right?

C B: Yes that is what I saw and then I noticed my dolls were gone. What am I going to do they are very fragile and very old and I have the birth certificate for each one of them. See no one keeps old things these days, and they are worth money.

Me: That is why they took them I bet.

C B: Or just to have something to take.

Me: Well that is just one way of thinking. This person could have thought that they were just playing dolls.

But they are worth a lot of money to the right person.

Me: If you are right you should go and take a small visit to this person that you think took them but don't say anything about the dolls.

C B: Okay! I can just go down for a few minutes and act like nothing has happened.

Me: Right can you do that.

C B: I think I can because we were friends for a long time.

Me: Well if you think you can get some information out of this person then go for it.

C B: Shilo come on and we will go for a walk.

Me: He is such a great dog and he knows who he likes and if he don't like you he will let you know right away. But Shilo will not come to you when you call for him. I think he is hard headed. But he is a good watch dog for her.

C B is good with Shilo and he is good for her. She has Cancer so he is a good friend.

Me: I have noticed every time some guy moves in guess who is the first one to see if they are single or not.

Switch hitter is always the first one to greet this person and go to his room to see what she can see and tell someone else what they can take when he is not in his room. That is teamwork. She tells shuffles what room and when he is not in there. She pulls out what she wants and they both go from there

Shuffles has a way of not saying anything all she does is moan, but that is just her way and she is good at it.

Even these cameras can't catch her. They are worthless.

Me: Well maybe we can get someone else in here to keep an eye on E. She is number two on the list of odd people to keep an eye on.

She is another one that plays games with the males she will hang around them and then she will say he raped me, just so someone will feel sorry for her.

But people are catching on to her ways, she is crying wolf way too often now people are not listening to her. She is just like Switch hitter. Fakes seizures and has these crazy people call an ambulance for her and they do it because it is her.

Me: Then we have people late at night coming in the side doors, they are here for a late night visit and drugs, they bring them in when most of us are in our rooms resting or sleeping, and a couple hours later they're sneaking out so they don't get caught.

So many people come and go here, it is pitiful to see. For an assisted living place it should be kept up better than it is and the people should be happier than they are.

I do think some of us are just thinking what we can do to improve this place. "Nothing. It is up to the slumlords."

They get all this money and spend it somewhere else.

But never here we all can prove that because nothing ever gets done that should be done. If I worked for the fire department this place would be either shut down or brought up to code.

But that will never happen here too many dollars and not enough cents. I think it is just for tax write off. The people that had it before were just as bad, they never put money into this place, and they were slumlords. Oh well, they are slumlords somewhere else now.

Well D L is on the move. He is out for boxes of gloves and whatever else he can take in his hand while driving his electric wheelchair and holding boxes of gloves.

On his way back to his room, no one sees anything and again the cameras are not working. Go figure it out.

I think if anyone ever wanted to buy this place and use it as a motel. They could make some money but only if they did a lot of changes to these room's because they really do need a lot of work.

They are already internet accessible and they are all ready for the TV to be plugged in, all they need is a rural fridge, all we have is a small fridge.

But no matter what if these people want anything they can just come on in and take whatever they want. This is the way it has been all along, no one cares, except the people that are missing things.

Someone told me earlier this week that some

rings from someone's room were missing and I also heard someone saying who took them.

I know who it is and I was not even there but I have seen the rings and they are on someone's hand, and I will not tell you who it is yet.

So if you think you know who took what did not belong to them say something, not like I can hear you but you would feel better I know.

I know I would feel better if these books could hear what you are thinking and saying. You know it is funny how some people do things in this place. If you have something that they want they just say it is theirs and that's the way it is.

They just take what is not theirs and you are called a thief because it is in your possession. You have to show a receipt for whatever it is that you have and they say it belongs to them. Proof is number one here not number two.

You know the people that work here don't even have to show up and get paid for it. To me this is wrong and they should put an end to it. See the people that are watching this place spend most of their time outside smoking. That is fine with me but they are just 2 feet from the building and that is a no no, according to the law, 10 feet or more outside a business but around here, it is, do whatever you want to do and get away with it, No problem.

That is the way it is here, no one is wrong. Everyone is right except you. See if you don't steal you are not good enough for their league.

Well I will never be good enough because I am a Detective and I have a lot more sense than their whole team.

When I went by somebody's room, they had the door open just far enough to see some pictures on the wall and I recognize them from someone else's room.

I asked where they came from and they said

I picked them up at a garage sale. I thought to myself I would have never seen anything like them before but that is what she told me and she looked right at the wall when she said it to me.

But once a thief always a thief, you cannot stop stealing just because someone thinks you should. That is not the way it goes people have to learn in time because you were not brought up that way, your family taught you better than that.

I have always heard I don't need your help. I can make it on my own. And that is what lead me to doing this. My family just leaves me alone and don't say a word about what I have done with my life.

I have seen things today that no one would believe and it is all one person that has done it and I was told that she is not the bad person in this caper.

But now I do know better. She has had the jewelry box all this time and this I know for sure because things do not just reappear all of the sudden.

Not even in this place it is never that easy, you have some good days and then you have bad days. In here you need to keep an eye on a lot of people and that is hard to do in here.

I was coming back to my room just last night and I saw Shuffles taking something that did not belong to her and yet no one ever sees this on camera because they are never pointing in the direction.

The camera is always pointed in another place never on the place it should be.

This is just a crazy place to live and I would never tell anyone to ever move in here. Unless you want everything taken from you and that is the way it is in here.

I am just saying that if you have something that is nice you don't want to move it in here because it will never be seen after you move in. I had some good things when I moved in here and they are gone. I have not got them back as of yet.

But maybe later on I will see them again, I hope, you never know. Stranger things have happened where I live. I think I have been trying to get out of here for as long as I have been here and that is to long, I have been here for 16 months.

I do everything myself, I go shopping, I pay my own bills I buy my own food. I take my own medicine and take my own showers. I make my own food and I am just here for the room and I do keep it clean. I have them do my laundry for me but that is all they do for me, I ask for nothing I even challenge myself to go to the store which I do on my electric wheelchair. I go to the store and get what I need and come back dodging cars and trucks to get back here.

I wish I had a way out of here because I have some plans for myself.

I just saw someone coming out of someone else's apartment with an arm load of things and it is only 7:45 PM. Where is everyone?

Apparently not in their rooms.

"Oh yes Bingo night."

Time for the caper here at the assisted living place I got it,

But I am watching everything that is going on around here,

And I do not lie about anything so I will turn this is at once like anyone cares. Probably not but it is my reputation that is going to get the flack because people do not come here for people but for stealing.

The cops have better things to do, other than drop things and come over here for a thief. That is the way the law thinks around here, don't call us we are too busy for this crap.

We have better things to do out here, not chase old people stealing.

Hey I have an idea, call a DETECTIVE AGENT THEY CAN HELP YOU.

They do all the stuff we can't do for you there.

When you call don't mention that you talked to us because that will make us look bad to other agencies.

Good then that is just what I am thinking of doing and then I will never forget to tell my team what to do if they ever run into something like this because of the police force acting so high and mighty.

This will knock them down a little bit and then we can get some things done properly.

This is what I should have done all along. I think this caper is just people that are not thinking with the right part of their mind, if they have a mind that is.

Believe me some of the people in here have no mind at all, they are. Just in here because the kids don't want to bother with them.

But some of us just have friends and no family.

Well the capers are still going on here, comes another nut down the hall with dishes and she is taking them to her room.

No wonder the dishes are disappearing all the time, and they can't find them.

All they have to do is go in to Shuffles room and they will find all kinds of dishes.

But her room is such a mess it might turn into a real job looking for them in there.

And they have some more people's room that they could check on cause I know for sure that Switch hitter has a lot of things that don't belong to her in her room.

But no one will check out the people that I mention to them. I think they are hoping I am wrong but I'm not.

I don't sleep much at night I like to write and watch other people and how they work out.

This is just one way to catch a thief, and a safe way,

Just ignore them and pretend they are invisible this way no one gets hurt.

See I have some things that other detectives don't have I have a brain to work with.

They just go on instinct and they don't imagine anything else. So see, I have the better part of this caper already I know how and they don't, and I have solved cases and they have just been doing nothing.

This is my way, I see and I do the rest on paper and tape. The police department is just a bunch of nerds and that is all they are and they get paid money for being stupid, imagine that.

Well I guess I need to go for my walk around this place and see what is going on inside and outside of here.

Wow it is a gathering of the smokers, intelligent people (the nerds).

What are they plotting this time? They are talking about stealing booze from someone that is a full time alcoholic, and he cannot be without his booze at all.

Good luck to these people because you start picking on an alcoholic, you are in for some pain.

I know for sure they are very angry people without their booze.

I have seen this most of my life, my step dad was a full time drunkard and he was a very angry person without his booze.

You could not even talk to him at all, or reason with him because he thought he was king of booze land and when he died he was a very sick person inside and out.

He made everyone's life miserable when he drank all the time. I think he died in 1975 I'm not sure.

He could steal anything while you were watching him, he was that good. Then he would ask where it came from.

But in here the people are so dunce that they think that the people in here are the people stealing from them, it is not the workers it is the people that live in here. And I have named them for you.

They are all named Shuffles / Switch hitter / E / Dumb Dumb D/ D S /Sky is C B.

C B: Is not too bad, she has her days, her and Shilo her watchdog.

He is so sweet and he will bite if he don't like you.

CB: Let's me know if things are looking bad and she would know cause she has been her longer than I have.

ME: See if I hear or see something going on. I can write it down and get the people that are involved with the missing things.

ME: I do have a keen eye for this kind of thing and that is why I am here. Cause I am good at my job, now and always.

Oh no! Here we go again the bitch from beyond is out and about I wonder who she is going to make her next fool. She has turned so many people in here against her for doing them wrong but she will cry if she is caught in a lie and get out of it.

The Bitch From Beyond: I didn't know what I did wrong but I think I was just doing what I thought was right.

Me: Yah sure you were, just stay away from me and my friends,

The Bitch from Beyond: I am not a bitch I am a good person to everyone. Ask anyone in here and they will tell you just how nice I am.

ME: Well let's see, you lie, cheat and cry if things are not going your way and you tell the people at the front desk I'm a bad person. So you are a real bitch and that is the truth.

The Bitch: Everyone likes me and that is the truth.

ME: Ok have it your way but I do know better you steal and then you say it is someone else taking from you, and it is not anyone. It is you. I know for sure that you have some gel pens for sharing and they ended up in your room where no one would be able to get them, and that is the truth. You are so much like the last owner here that you all don't know what the truth is. You have lied so much you don't know the truth.

The Bitch from Beyond: You are wrong I have never lied to you and you know this is true.

ME: That is all you have done since I got here, I think if you ever told the truth you would probably have to go back to the crying thing and that will get you better results because I don't fall for this crap from you or anybody.

The Bitch: I am not a bitch, I am just me, a liar and a cheat.

ME: And you have so much crap in your room that no one can move around in there but I do know one thing and that is that you will get some jail time out of this and I will not hold back when your time is here. That is a promise, and I am good a carrying out my promises.

The Bitch: You can't say that to me and get away with it,

I have never been so humiliated in my life.

ME: Just hang in there you are young yet, you have a lot of time ahead of you. You can do this I know for sure that is up to your speed.

The Bitch: Why are you so mean to me I haven't done anything to you, Have I?

ME: Oh let's see you, lied to me, you stole from me and you are a Bitch to me. So you figure it out, okay? You know if you did not try and tell everyone that you are queen of this place you might have some friends and stop trying to run everything, you are not the boss of anything other than yourself that is all. No one cares, you are holding up your name very well, Bitch and I say that with respect and I mean every word.

We can't all be as bitchy as you can because we do respect our elders and you are not one of them. Or you would try and be a nicer person for a while but I know that is a lot to look forward to, knowing you and your reputation.

See why this is called the twist and turns of the heist, because the plot changes all the time. I never know where I am going with it, I just go and then I see something like shuffles carrying something's that are not hers.

Pictures off the wall going to her room, they will never be seen again because her room is a total mess. You can ask anybody and they will tell you just how much a mess it is.

Wow, here comes a cool guy. He is so sweet and he keeps to himself. There is never any trouble from him, he is just a good young guy mike. He is an ex-cop and very bright and he hates this place almost as much as I do.

Mike: Wow! Did you see Shuffles taking pictures down to her room?

ME: Oh yes I saw her and I heard her deep rough voice coming down the hall.

Mike: So how many pictures are missing so far, because I see 5 at her door?

ME: I have an idea that they are very hot and from someone else's room, don't you agree?

Mike: I have not seen anything gone from the walls yet.

I am going for a stroll in the complex you want to go with me?

ME: Well, I see where they are coming from the look in here someone is just moving in and did not lock the door.

Mike: So Shuffles just came in and took what she wanted and her she comes again.

ME: What are you doing making a phone call?

Mike: Yes I am to the police department to see what is going on in here.

ME: You know they will not do anything right.

Mike: Yes but this way it is on record and filed

with a date and time and where it all took place so I am happy.

ME: I know what you are saying but nothing is as it appears, remember that okay? Because things fall into the wrong hands at the police department. I know this because it has happened to me more than one time, and for some reason the file just gets misplaced somehow, and I think I need to find out where and why things are going.

Mike: You are looking for some reasoning you are looking in the wrong place. These cops are dumb and young, they are not out to help us old retired cops. I do remember you are not a cop you were a Sheriff.

ME: And that means I should get to the bottom of the problem here and find out why things are here one time and gone the next time. That should never happen in a police station no matter what. I was always told we are out to protect and serve.

Mike: That is almost like the post office, say one thing and do another.

ME: Rain, hail, snow or sleet, we shall do our rounds, to get the job done.

But protect and serve, is our police motto, protect the people and serve the people but that is not happening anymore so what is going on.

Mike: I have no idea I always kept my eye out for the rest of the night when I was working and everything ran smoothly I just don't know what has happened. They are not friendly anymore they treat you like crap.

ME: I am so glad my sheriff's office is not. Like that they respect everyone who comes through the door and this crime spree would not be going on it would have come to a head a long time ago. The people would be behind bars for a long time no matter what age they are. My department has respect for the people here and California.

I think all countries and counties should show respect to everyone. That is just my way of thinking.

Shy: I know something that happen earlier today ole Shuffles took a fall after one beer with a friend of hers, and refuse to go to the Hospital, she looks a little red in the face but she will heal and then she will be back to acquire more stuff that don't belong to her once a thief always a thief, that is the way it goes for some people.

ME: Yes I know this is true and I have seen a lot of it in my 70 some odd years and it is always the same, people ever do change because they always want something that don't belong to them. I always ask myself, "Why don't they work and get what they want?" Instead they think it is easier to acquire it from someone else.

Even though it is wrong, that is what they do and they think it is right and the funny thing about living here is that the workers here see nothing and know nothing.

They just go about their way and let things go, remember the fraze hear no evil. See no evil. Speak no evil, well that is the way it is here.

Shy: Hay look who is coming down the hall. It is Switch hitter with E. They are plotting something because they are too close to just be talking about someone else in here. Funny thing is that Switch hitter has been with some real wieners in her days and yet she hangs on to the biggest whore in this place.

They follow each other around like they are glued together. They live together and he gets what he wants, and his laundry's done every day, and that's what keeps him happy.

Mike: Have you seen E coming down the hall, she has another jewelry box that she has acquired from my neighbor's apartment but not from D S this time. She is walking on very thin ice with a lot of people in this place and I can see why.

She just stares at you non-stop, and that is just so stupid.

She should be somewhere else but not here in a mental place where she has more friends just like her.

ME: I think we all agree with that she is kind of freaky, and she is always lingering about the hall looking for someone else to follow around. I just saw a great big vase going down the hallway, and it had legs. The vase was bigger than Shuffles, but it made it back to her room. These new people that are moving in are not going to have anything left.

They did not lock their door so she is just helping herself to everything that she can.

Mike: "Oh my goodness!" I see the new people coming in the door and Shuffles is going to be caught. We hope so anyway, damn they missed her and she is in her room just in time.

I am going by the room and I hear someone say where all our stuff is? I stop and tell these people to lock your door all the time or you will have nothing at all. They said all our pictures and vases are gone and clothes and jewelry box is all gone. "Do you have any idea where it all went to?"

You need to go down to the office and they

will help you out.

ME: Hey Mike, "what is going on down here? Anything new?"

Mike: You mean other than the people getting ripped off, no more than usual. I just told these new people to go to the office and get help. Someone took all their things from their room.

"Go figure huh".

ME: Yeah, and the office people are behind a lot of this crap that is walking away. They will tell you to call the police and file a report, but they will not do anything. Damn, I love my job. It's the best job in the world being a detective. I love it. The assisted living capers, which is such a great name for this job.

Mike: At least you came up with a good name for this book. And the capers are true, well most of them are true.

ME: I just wish it was all over so I could go back home where I belong. I miss my home so much you could not guess. The weather is so much better than here. I have been here way to long and I still feel out of place. It will never get better no matter what I do because I have tried everything.

Mike: Well, I will miss you when you leave here and that's the truth. I feel like we have known each other for some time now and you are good company.

ME: Well thank you Mike and that is very sweet of you to say that to me. You are a one of a kind guy and I will miss you a lot but I'm not gone yet and it was nice of you to work with me on this book and you have never seen anything like this before right. You have been there to watch what is going on all around this place, I just bet you have seen more in here than you did out on the streets.

Mike: Well let's just say it is never boring in this place when you are watching someone get their place robbed because they did not lock their door on their room. It sucks because this place has cameras and they are never pointed in the direction they should be. Here comes Shuffles again and she looks like she went on a fight and did not know how to protect herself and yet she is looking for someone to leave there room unlocked so she can go in and rip them off.

ME: I saw what she looked like and she looked bad but today she looks like she had a very painful night just looking at her face. Oh no! Here comes the other two. Switch hitter and E what a pair to draw too. You know these three should be on an Island somewhere far away from civilization that would almost make life bearable for some of us.

Mike: That would be too much for them, they are all morons and I know some of the people here would miss them a lot just ask around and they will say yes we would miss them all a lot.

Sky And Shilo: The dog that barks at the drop of a hat. If he don't like you then he will let you know it. He will grill and bark, just don't put your hand down at him because he will bite.

He will as he is just because he is protecting his owner. That is what a dog is for and to take care of the home.

Mike: I have seen him get all bent out of shape and that is hard for Shilo to do but he don't care because he has never been around kids. I think maybe it is that they are too loud for him. I have seen kids kick dogs and treat them like crap. I can see that happening and Shilo has an instinct about people.

ME: Well I don't blame the dog for protecting his owner but if a kid comes running at the dog I would do the same thing and no questions asked. Anyway, I got most of what I needed from the front desk. If her Pepsi's are gone there is going to be hell to pay and they know nothing at all. I think they do, they are just not talking but that is normal here.

Sky: I did see somebody coming down the hall and it was Shuffles and E the team that stays together and they always will, I bet, all three of them are very odd people.

ME: Dan, He will steal something while you are watching him and then just take it to his room and they say nothing to him about it at all. There is something wrong with this place it is not just me that can see what is going on and no one will do anything about it. This place sucks big time and that is no bull shit.

I have seen him take gloves pins toilet paper towels anything you can imagine he takes coffee cups and leaves them outside and sugar and creamers. We had some decorations for the holidays and he took some of them for his room and his chair. I myself think he is a thief because nothing ever comes back. He keeps everything, I call him hot fingers Dan.

Mike: Then we have a great jackass DS. He is the biggest jackass in this place and it will never change till he is gone. He raises he'll about things that are missing and he bitches about the food and he smokes with the door open by his room. He bitches about his girlfriend all the time about the money he don't get. It is all just a bunch of bullshit, he buys all these old electric wheelchairs and he thinks he can fix them up (not) but he buys them anyway and he wonders where his money goes. Other than his girlfriend stealing from him. She always has his money and she is always in his room and she is in other men's rooms also checking to see what she can steal. If you ever brought a police dog in here he would go crazy. It would not know what way to go and find the drugs and other stolen things.

ME: Then we have everybody in here mad about the staff that will not take them to town because they say the bus is broke. There is no one to drive it, everything in this place is a pain in the ass. No respect from anyone in here. The workers are a pain in the ass they are just all for themselves. You cannot get good workers these days.

Maybe what I have heard is true, they don't get paid enough to work in this place. Shit as lousy as the food is here. I am smart, I don't eat the food in here. I buy my own and eat in my room. No one would steal food from here if you are looking to stay alive for another year we hope.

Sky: Have you seen Shilo? He ran out the door and I cannot find him.

M E: I sure have, he has someone down at the end of the hall cornered. From taking something out of someone else's apartment that he knows, and guess who it is Shuffles, he sure doesn't like her.

Sky: Oh my gosh Shilo are you ok buddy? I was so worried about you. I forgot to lock my door, come on and get up her on the walker and we will go and lock the door and go for a walk. Wow, outside is very nice today and that was quite a job you did young man. Getting someone for stealing something from someone else's room. You are a very good watch dog. Know everyone will know who you are, my little watchdog in the assisted living capers.

This is just so cool I love it, Shilo you are a one of a kind dog and you are mine and I love you forever little one.

Mike: What is going on down here I heard a lot of people down the hall and some barking but I can't see around corners yet. I did recognize the bark Shilo right and he must have seen someone that he don't like and he knows who is doing the stealing around here. He would be a great police dog but he knows too many good people in here. He would have to be trained to find whatever we were looking for drugs, people or whatever, you know what I am saying. Not one person in here could ever say anything about Shilo doing his job. If they did not know he was an undercover worker for the police department he would have to be paid to do his job otherwise they are just showing off a great dog and his talent and to me that is wrong, no one should ever take advantage of a dog or a person.

ME: Hey Mike, how are you and how are things going? I have been told that we have a watch dog on duty huh.

Let me guess it must be Shilo because he is a very bright dog and he has lots of friends in here, so who did he take down?

Sky: Well he caught shuffles taking something

from someone's apartment and it did not belong to her and he cornered her so she could not get away. I love him and told him what a good dog he was. He is a very smart dog and a very good watch dog he knows who he likes and who he don't like. He is so lovable to most people except ones that he don't like Shuffles he just don't care for her at all I guess.

ME: Wow I guess I need to keep more dog treats in my place for Shilo huh. He is such a good boy and a great friend to all the people that he likes. He is a caper stopper, he needs to be on watch to keep Shuffles in her place and not out lingering in the halls, make her stay in her room.

We lock our doors and she still tries to get in, she is looking for free sodas or something else to take back to her room. She is a pain in the ass, and this place cannot do anything about it. To me, that is a lot of bullshit and we should have more say so than what we do but no one here can do anything they say, and I think they should turn her into a place where they can treat her for what she has been doing for some time. She needs to be stopped.

There is another one that is a real pain in the butt, and her name is (E), she is a real winner she likes to stalk people and then just stare at them all the time, she never stops, she is a stalker to me, that is what we call them at the sheriff's office and I am sure it has not changed. Between these two and Switch hitter we have more trouble than we need in one place. They are all members of the gang in this place. The assisted living capers, they are the capers, and they think that they will never get caught.

I knew who they were when I first got in here. I am a detective and I also know what to look for in people.

Believe me these three stand out in a crowd and that is saying a lot about any one in here because they are not all in their right minds, some of us are sane and some are insane, but we are where we should not be.

Anyway, I for one will be so glad when I can travel again. Just away from here would make a big difference to me, don't get me wrong, I have a roof over my head and I have some friends and I have my books, and I can write. Other than that I am doing great. I am just here to watch the thieves and it is so funny to watch them, they act like they are space cadets because the three walk around like they are all spaced out. They don't see beyond their nose but that is not a shock for this place. Some of the people cannot see beyond their noses this place will do that to you and some of the people that you thought were cool were just putting you on. I know better now I know all the odd balls from the paranormal and me. I think I am normal but I wonder what is normal anymore.

You do not even the workers are normal. They are all paranormal people too but they get paid to act like assholes to us and get away with it and this is the truth. Some of the workers in here don't care about you they just want the money that they get to make them feel better, not you.

Sky: I just saw something that you can never believe. It is Switch hitter, she is taking some someone's Pepsi to her room and she did not even ask for it. She was trying to run across the yard to her place and hide the Pepsi's. They are a friend of mines sodas so she better bring them back to me or I will get them myself and I know where they belong.

ME: Sky, what is going on out there I just saw someone trying to run across the yard with something. I could not make out what it was, did you see who it was or did I imagine it, I never know any more.

Mike: Hey there ladies, what is going on? I just saw something that I have never seen before. Someone is trying to run with a walker and a seat full of sodas. I can imagine who it was but I think you all know who it was right?

Sky: Yes it was Switch hitter and she had Pepsi in her chair. I am sure she did not pay for it because it was still on the crate. I think it belong to a friend I will not say who but you know as well as I do, who it belongs to, and she is going to be very upset if it came from her room because she loves her Pepsi's. Her Pepsi's are the most important thing to her and if her Pepsi's are gone from her room there is going to be hell to pay. I know this for a fact.

The morale to this story is don't trust anyone no matter who it is. If they come to you and say that they are a friend or foe don't trust them in your room in your home or wherever. Just do for you don't trust nobody.

I know I only trust a couple of my friends. See everyone is out to make a buck and they don't care who they hurt to make that buck but you don't get anything out of it except a bad time and ranking from other people that try to warn you before. Anything really bad can happen. Just do me a favor if you have a friend that wants to always do something for you, check this person out first because you never know when people are going to change. Believe me people do have a great chance to change if you have known them for a long time and some of the changes are not for the good. There are some in this world that want to make a living off of good people like you and I but it can get expensive and just think you are paying for it.

I do have friends that want anything that they can get their hands on and I try to stay as far away from them as possible and so far it has worked and I hope it will for a long time to come.

Dee: See the reason for this book is a warning to people in a place like assisted living places because they are out here just for ripping people off. This place that I live in is the number one place not to live. I can tell you there is one in Sheridan Oregon but I can't give you the name of the assisted living place. Though if you ask around you will find out all kinds of things about it.

If you do drugs and you steal, this is the place

for you.

Otherwise you need to find something that is more affordable for your family and you. Friendly people help, someone you can talk to. Friendly people are hard to find anymore and finding a place that you are going to feel safe and being safe makes a large difference.

You want to be where you can trust people and leave your room unlocked when you go somewhere. Like going to the store and coming back and everything is still in your place and not somewhere else. Just to be honest, assisted living sucks big time.

This is the voice of experience, I have been here 16 months and they have done nothing but lie to me from the beginning and that right there is wrong. They told me I was close to a store and it is a mile and a half to the market in town but McMinnville is 20 miles from here and that is where I do my shopping and I have to call a ride one day early to go to town and you have as long as you want if you tell them what time you want to come back, they will be there.

Well ride has some very good drivers, and they have respect for you. See, I am in a wheelchair and they are very nice to me but I know a lot of the drivers from the 12 companies that work for well ride and they are all super cool people, I have met a couple I did not care for but not too many.

Any way, if you live in Oregon please check out the place that you are moving in. It could turn out to be like this place and that I would not wish on my enemy. I hope I don't have any of them but I think you know what I am saying just be careful please. Go online and check it out,

I know you don't know me but I am a very honest person who cares about what happens to you and your family.

See, I write true stories and I write fictional stories.

I love to write, so if I am asking you to do something then there is a very good reason for it.

Well, the Twist and Turns of the heist is my first book,

And this one is The Twist and Turns of The heist 2

The Assisted Living Capers. You will get such a kick out of it and it is so true. Well most of it is true. I can't use real people's names so I used some fictitious names and it suits them to a tee. The dog that is his real name Shilo, he is just a year old and quite a sweet dog, he is tan and white and very little black on him.

There is a picture of him in this book he is just so sweet. He is the kind of dog that needs to be around kids. Shilo has never been around kids but he sure knows who his friends are and I have pictures in this book that are of the property.

Here to tell you all the truth I am suppressed. Nothing has come up missing from outside yet, it is in the garden shed that don't look very well and yet it is all still there.

Any way I caught the 5 Bad people in this book and I found everything that was taken in a storage place just up the street and I looked inside and everything was in there.

Everything that was taken from assisted living was found in the storage place. The 5 people that were involved are back at the place and not a word is said about anything that happened.

The people that got ripped off got all their stuff back and no questions asked. I have done the capers before not here but in California and it was a real caper it was a house full of furniture that was taken from the house.

They had cameras on and yet nobody saw anything, the same as here. All is well on its way back to the assisted living. You know what all I got for this is a bad time.

Well Enjoy and thanks for reading! (Dee)

-THE END-

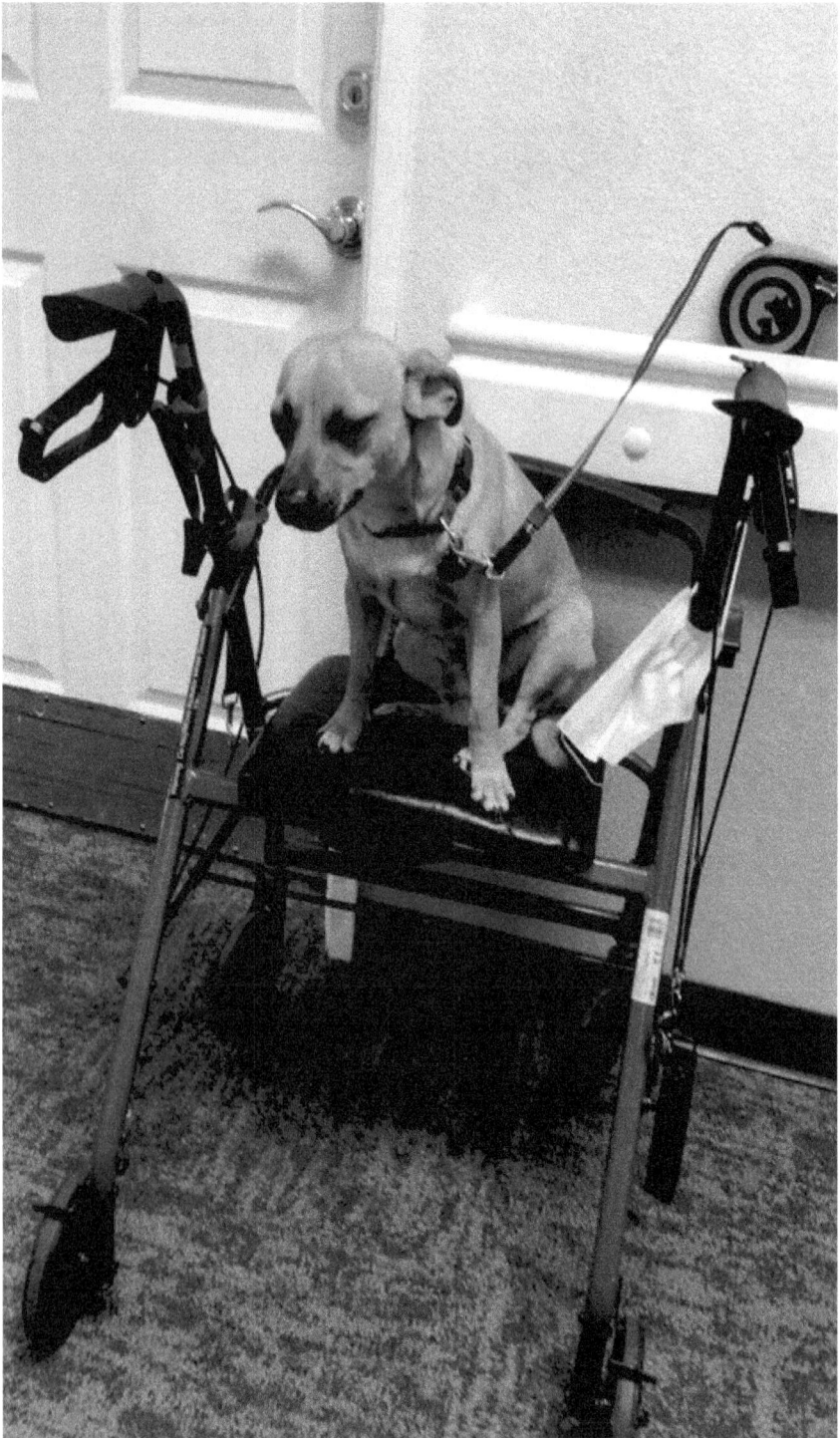

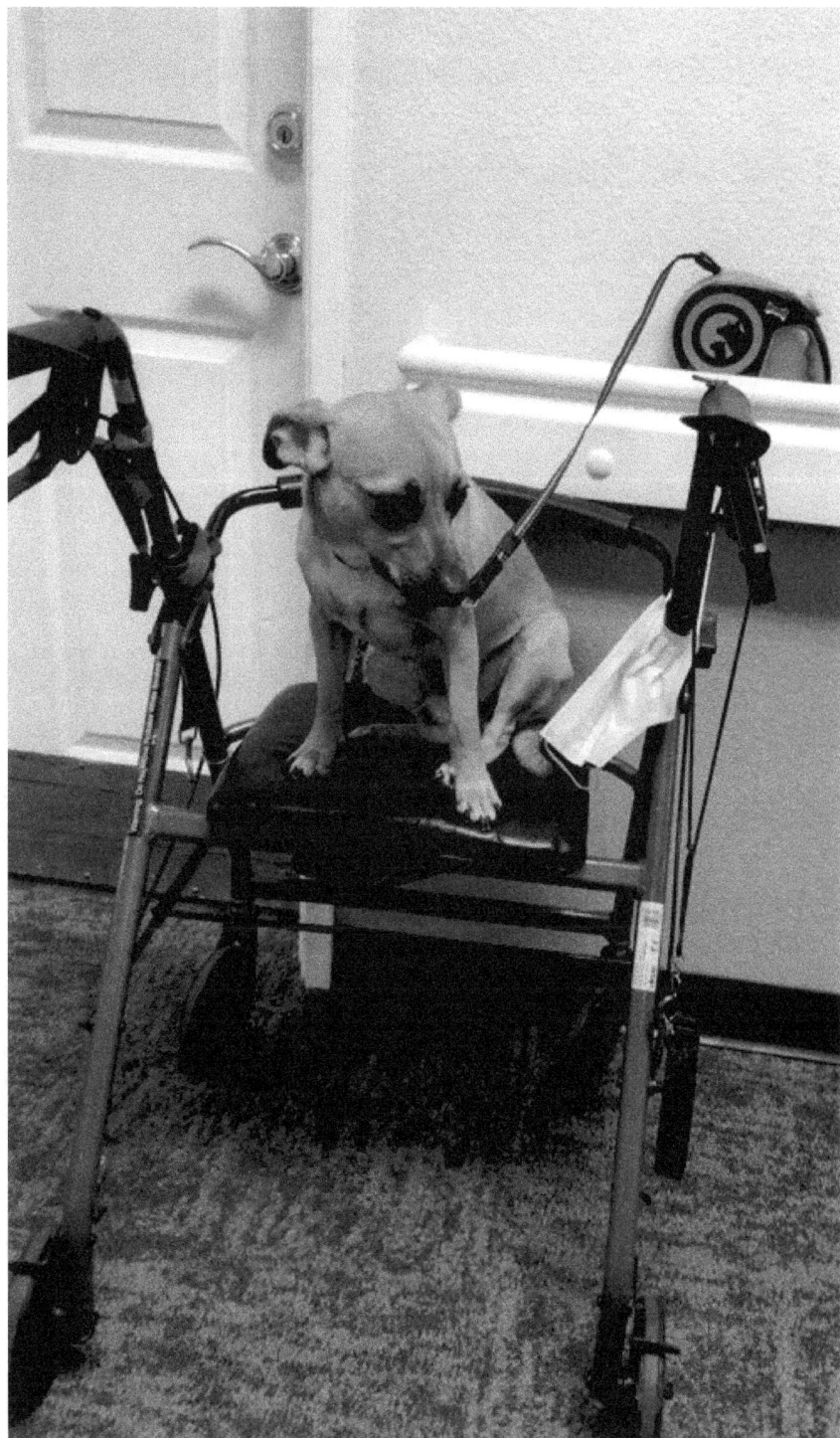

CPSIA information can be obtained
at www.ICGtesting.com
Printed in the USA
BVHW081009140323
660404BV00007B/475

9 798886 228588